SEREE'S STORY

IRMA GOLD & WAYNE HARRIS

WALKER BOOKS
AND SUBSIDIARIES
LONDON • BOSTON • SYDNEY • AUCKLAND

For Hamish, fellow ele lover, and
for Lek Chailert, elephant whisperer
and superwoman. IG

For Beverly and Jeannette,
and for all our mothers. WH

First published in 2022
by Walker Books Australia Pty Ltd
Locked Bag 22, Newtown
NSW 2042 Australia
www.walkerbooks.com.au

A catalogue record for this
book is available from the
National Library of Australia

ISBN: 978 1 925126 99 0

The illustrations for this book were hand drawn
and painted directly to a digital platform

Typeset in Rockwell
Printed and bound in China

Seree loved rolling in the mud
and spraying it onto her back.
The delicious squelch and splatter of it.

Seree loved eating
bananas by the dozen.
The sweet golden
mush of them.

But most of all,
Seree loved walking with the herd.
The sound of her grandmother
and aunties rumbling around her,
the squeaks of her naughty cousins,
and always her mother, right beside her.
Life was good.

But not for long.
When they came,
the herd scattered in fright,
their trumpeting calls
shattering the morning.
Seree and her mother
were cornered.

Trunks outstretched,
for just a moment,
the very tips of them touched.
One last kiss.

Seree was put to work
in the circus.
She lived her life in chains,
and three times a day
she was made to perform.

She danced on her hind legs.
She walked a tightrope.
She kicked a soccer ball.
She threw darts at a balloon.

When the shows were done
and the crowds had gone,
Seree was left alone.
She rocked from side to side
and thought of her family.

She thought of her grandmother and aunties,
and all her little cousins.
But most of all, she thought of her mother.
In her dreams, she escaped to the herd,
her mother always right beside her.

Years passed,
but Seree's life never changed.
The crowds came,
the crowds went.
Seree's heart grew tighter
and tighter.
All she looked forward to
was the freedom of sleep.
But always she woke in chains.

The night Seree's heart
was at its lowest,
three strangers approached.
Seree sensed them
before she saw them.
The hairs on her spine prickled.
But their touch was soft.
They fed her treats,
long-forgotten flavours.
And whispered promises
in her ears.

Kind hands offered watermelon
and pumpkin and corn stalks.
In between mouthfuls,
Seree waved her trunk in the air.

As Seree stepped off the truck,
she tasted the air.
It was perfumed with
the smell of long ago.
The smell of happiness.
The smell of belonging.
Mud and bananas and other elephants.
Lots of them.

They trundled towards her.
They nuzzled her.
And for the first time
in a very long time,
Seree's heart unclenched.

Then a sound filled the air.
She stopped.
She listened. She ran.

And there she was.
Seree stroked behind her ears,
along her spine, under her belly,
rumbling softly all the while.
Her mother. Life was good.

ABOUT ELEPHANTS

Endangered

At the start of the twentieth century (1900 CE) there were over 100,000 Asian elephants living in the wild. Now they are an endangered species, and there are only about 35,000 Asian elephants left in the entire world. In Thailand, there are only about 2000 left in the wild, with another 2000 in captivity.

Food and drink

Elephants need to eat about 200 to 300 kilograms of food, and drink 100 to 200 litres of water every day. (Humans only eat about 2.5 kilograms of food and drink 2 litres of water a day!) Their trunks can hold 6 litres of water. That's about the same as four full kettles!

Elephants are vegetarian. They love to eat bananas, bamboo, berries, sugar cane, mangoes, wild rice, coconuts, corn, melon and jungle shrubs.

Did you know?

The elephant is the largest animal on land.

A newborn elephant calf weighs 90 kilograms.

Elephants have the biggest ears of any animal.

Elephants' trunks are boneless but have 100,000 muscles, are 2 metres long and weigh about 140 kilograms.

Elephants make their own sunscreen! They coat themselves in water and dirt to protect their skin.

In the wild

Elephants have deep family bonds and live in herds led by the oldest female, who is called the matriarch. Female elephants stay together their whole lives. Male elephants, or bulls, leave the herd at about 13 and usually live alone, but sometimes they form small groups with other bulls.

In captivity

Every elephant around the world used for entertainment has been through a process called the "phajaan", or "crushing". At the age of two, they are taken from their mothers and put in the "crush box". They are beaten until their spirits are broken and they are ready to serve humans.

Captive elephants in Thailand work in illegal logging or in camps and circuses where they perform tricks and take tourists for rides. Elephants often work for 12 to 15 hours a day carrying people on their backs. When they are not working, elephants are constantly chained, usually by both front feet. This means that throughout their entire lives they may never lie down. Asian elephants live for about 70 years.

You can help

You can become a voice for elephants. Tell others why they should not ever ride an elephant, watch a circus or buy an elephant painting. If you visit Asia, only visit a genuine sanctuary where they do not offer any of these activities or use bullhooks to control their elephants.

Elephant Nature Park (ENP), founded by Lek Chailert, is an amazing sanctuary in Chiang Mai, Thailand, where you can spend time with over 80 rescued elephants. Visit elephantnaturepark.org

After rescue

Like Seree, some elephants are reunited with their mothers after they are rescued. But most are not so lucky and never see their families again. At ENP they develop bonds with other elephants and form new herds. There, they can splash in the river, roll in the mud and eat bananas to their hearts' content.

Freedom

"Seree" means "freedom". All elephants have the right to live free and safe from harm.